Shadow
of
Danger

KRISTINE MASON

ISBN: 1490901809
ISBN-13: 9781490901800

For my mom, Joan.

Thank you for being a wonderful mother and friend.
For believing in me.
For encouraging my imagination.
I miss you.

ACKNOWLEDGMENTS

Special thanks to Jamie Denton, Christy Carlson and Mary Ann Chulick. Thank you for all of your help and advice! Big shout out to my cover artist Kim Van Meter, KD Designs.

PROLOGUE

Twelve years earlier...

"NOW WHAT ARE we going to do with her?"

The trace of amusement in Garrett's voice had him pausing mid-buckle. The man was a depraved, sick fuck, and today, he'd dragged him into hell.

And he liked it. Loved it. Knew he'd crave it again and again. The struggle, the fight, the dominance.

He ignored Garrett and focused on finishing zipping and buckling his pants. An effort considering his hands were clammy and swollen, covered in blood, and shaking from the adrenaline still pumping through his veins.

"Well," Garrett drawled. "Whaddya say, *Toby*?"

Garrett was the only one who called him by that name, and he hated himself for loving the way Garrett's voice rushed over him, caressed him. Hated himself for wanting something so twisted and immoral.

Instead of answering, he stared at the naked woman on the floor. Her groans were muffled by the dish towel they'd stuffed into her mouth earlier. Blood flowed from her nose and now covered the pears and apples design on the old rag. Her cheeks had doubled in size and were already purpling. One of her eyes had swollen shut, while the other remained nothing but a watery, puffy slit. Bite marks, and black and blue handprints, which could have been either his or Garrett's—didn't matter—marred her pale, nude body. His dick hardened at a sight that should have horrified him. But the memory of the way he'd taken her, the forbidden way, the way no woman had ever allowed him, was so damned fresh in his mind, he could still feel it.

"Toby," Garrett murmured. "Wanna take her again?"

He finally looked at Garrett. He tried to ignore his wide shoulders, muscular chest, and the sheen of sweat coating the other man's massive biceps. He couldn't, though. Not with the way Garrett's big dick twitched and hardened as he lay sprawled on the ratty sofa staring at the woman.

He grabbed Garrett's jeans from the floor and tossed them to him, then looked at the whore they'd spent the afternoon playing with in disgust. No, he didn't want her again. But he did want another just like her. Still, Garrett was right, what the hell were they going to do with her now?

She'd seen their faces, knew their names. She might be some white trash, gutter whore, but if she went to the cops, the long arm of the law would hunt them down, which seemed like a big waste of taxpayer dollars to him. Whores deserved shit. They deserved to rot in hell, every last one of them. Selling their bodies for drugs, or to pay a few bills, maybe feed their bastard kids, or make rent in some hellhole not fit for a fucking cockroach. Did their plump little whore have any bastard kids hanging around, hungry and living in filth? Did she use them for her drugs, for her money, for her slutty clothes?

Fury, so sweet and raw, clawed inside him, settled low in his gut and made his dick swell with something more than sexual excitement. He knelt down and pulled the towel from her mouth. He knew what to do with her. Knew what she deserved, what every whore deserved. But did he have the nerve?

Garrett launched off the couch, shoving his long legs into his jeans. "What the hell are you doing, you stupid ass? If that bitch screams my neighbors will hear."

"They won't hear shit. Her jaw's broken, and she's barely conscious. Ain't that right?" He knocked her head with the back of his hand. Her one eye rolled back, but her ragged moan had him nearly coming on the spot. Yeah, he liked this new power, how it invigorated him, breathed life into his dismal existence.

As Garrett moved closer, he forced his gaze to the corner of the room. Trying desperately to keep his eyes off of the other man and the way he looked shirtless, his jeans hanging open. He'd been told, too many times over the years, that he wore his emotions on his sleeve. What he was feeling now, Garrett could never discover. Ever. He'd kill him if he knew.

"She's seen us and knows where I live," Garrett snarled as he looked down at the whore. "If she's found here, we'll have cops all over our asses. So..." He shrugged and smiled. A slow, easy, arousing smile. "I guess we'll just have to make sure she can't talk, won't we?"

He hated the way that smile made his dick even harder. But he hated the woman even more for not being able to satisfy his true lust.

He looked down at her again. Garrett was right. They couldn't afford to allow her to walk away—to live. And knowing Garrett as he did, he knew the man could and would fix this for them.

Garrett draped an arm over his shoulder. "It was a hell of an afternoon, huh?"

He merely grunted. Garrett's close proximity, his touch made it difficult for him to speak.

"Yep, I think we got something good going today, don't you?"

He turned his head and stared at Garrett who continued to look at the woman. His dark, gray eyes sizzled with something akin to lust as another one of his sensual smiles worked his firm lips.

"This wasn't supposed to happen. It can't happen again," he said, the whine in his voice grating on his own nerves.

"Why not? I know you liked it. Man, you should have seen

your face when you fucked her plump ass. You telling me you don't want to do that again?" Garrett drew him closer and whispered in his ear. "Beat that bitch? Fuck that ass until everything drains from you. Until *you've* drained *her?*"

He did like it. The rush. The power. The vengeance.

Hating and loving the way Garrett held him, he slowly nodded and forced himself to move away. "I did, but we can't do this again. I can't have the heat coming down on me."

"Don't be such a pussy." Garrett slapped him on the back. "I've been at this for a while, but after seeing you in action, I'm thinking maybe we could make this a real team effort."

When he met his gaze, Garrett shrugged. "I know how to get rid of her. I know how to keep a secret safe."

Of that, he knew damned well. Garrett had been keeping their secrets safe for many years. But he could be stupid at times. His arrogance, his cockiness, could land them into a whole lot of shit. He stared at the woman again, his pulse racing at what Garrett had proposed. *They* could do this again, and again. Keep their secrets to themselves. Enjoy the high, the moment together. He wanted that. The special bond. *The secret.*

His mind drifted back to that God awful night. The night that had changed him, and made him want something he shouldn't. And he had a sudden, overwhelming realization of what he needed to maintain his sanity, to maintain the charade.

This afternoon might not have given him what he'd truly wanted, what he'd never tell Garrett or anyone else on the planet, but it gave him a substitute. Sodomizing the whore while staring into Garrett's eyes had given him the next best thing, a sexual release he'd never find in the privacy of his own bedroom with his girlfriend. She, Garrett, no one would understand those dark, sexual demons. Something he didn't understand himself.

"Fine," he said, controlling the enthusiasm rushing through his veins. "Do what you have to do, to make this go away."

"Uh-uh," Garrett grunted. Moving to the end table, he ripped the cord from the lamp, then wrapped it around the whore's throat. He offered him one end of the cord. "We do this together. On the count of three, you understand me? We do this together."

He took the end of the cord, looked down at the whore, who moaned in pain and protest, then smiled. He was more than ready to do whatever it took to make his brother proud.

CHAPTER 1

Present day...

FINGERS CLAWING AT the sheets, tearing them from the mattress, Celeste Risinski woke with a scream. Panicked, disoriented, she shoved at hands she swore still gripped her. As she struggled, she knocked the alarm clock from the nightstand. When it hit the hardwood floor, the radio blared. The loud music, laced with crackling static, startled her.

She whipped open her eyes, relief slowing her racing heart as she looked down at her body, to where her arms and legs were tangled in the thin sheets and comforter. Brutal hands weren't holding her down. She wasn't in the woods. She wasn't fighting for her life. She was in her bedroom, waking up from another nightmare, another look into hell.

Dragging in a deep breath, she pulled herself to the edge of the mattress, bent and retrieved the clock. After turning off the radio, she placed it back on the nightstand, then wiped tears from her face she didn't remember crying.

No, not true. In her nightmare, she'd cried and screamed, begged and pleaded, while trapped in the body of another woman. She hated the way her mind had been sucked into the woman's soul. She'd experienced every ounce of the terror, and even the pain the woman had endured. She rubbed her neck where the phantom cord had been wrapped during the dream. Even though she was blessedly free of the nightmare and sitting in her bedroom, claustrophobia wrapped tightly around her, making it difficult to breathe.

She fought off the weight of the deadly illusion, and forced herself off the bed. With the dream still fresh in her mind, she grabbed the pen and pad of paper from her nightstand, sat back on the bed and began writing, just as she had the past three mornings. Her hands shook as she wrote, making her already terrible handwriting worse.

This nightmare, this vision had seemed more real than the others, almost more personal. Which was ridiculous considering she'd never had a premonition or psychic vision about herself.

The woman in her dream wasn't her. That woman had pretty hands, long nails perfectly manicured and painted blood red. She looked at her fingers gripping the pen, raw from constantly scrubbing, cleaning, and baking, her nails short and bare of color. Then she shuddered as the memory of the woman's red nails, snapping back when she'd clawed the dirt and fought for survival, rolled through her mind.

She jotted that piece of information on the paper as well, along with every other detail she remembered. The woods, the clearing she'd run through during the dream. The sounds the night creatures had croaked, wailed and chattered. The hum of cars along a highway, the scent of rubber and tar. God, the vile, putrid smell of body odor from the killer as he had held her against his chest.

She knew in her gut he *had* killed the woman. She rubbed her neck again. She might have woken right before witnessing the murder, but deep in her heart she knew the woman was dead. Almost as if the woman's death had left a black mark on Celeste's soul. A permanent tattoo no plastic surgeon could ever erase.

She might never be able to rid herself of the violent images, but she could share them. So she wrote quickly, no detail too small. If she'd actually witnessed the deaths of these women in her dreams, her notes might help to either find their bodies or find their killer.

Once finished, she drew in a deep breath, set the pad and pen on the nightstand, and forced herself off the bed. Four nights with barely any sleep, her body protested moving, and her mind...she couldn't seem to think straight anymore. She'd gone from content and carefree to a bundle of terrified nerves. She'd become afraid to close her eyes, afraid that if she did, she'd have another vision.

At least she'd woken in her bed this morning, she thought as she moved her leaden feet into the bathroom, then turned on the shower faucet. After the first nightmare, she'd woken up in her bathtub, thankfully empty of water. After the second nightmare, in the basement, and after the third, in the kitchen underneath the table, her arms and legs tangled in the wooden legs. Her nightmares were physically controlling her body, and that lack of control scared the hell out of her. What if she'd woken up lying in the middle of Main Street? Or in Old Lady Turner's flowerbed?

She groaned and stepped under the hot spray of water. The gossip from her next door neighbor alone would have everyone in town knowing her business and confirming her eccentricities. And she hated how some people, the people who didn't understand, looked at her.

She wasn't eccentric, she was...different. Her mother had raised her to embrace her quirky qualities, as well as her gift. Unfortunately, her gift, her ability to predict events through her dreams, had become a curse. Vivid, horrifying nightmares of rape and murder.

If only her mom were still alive. She'd had the gift, too. Maybe she could explain these visions, why they'd become so intense and frightening. But her mother was dead, buried in the small cemetery just outside of town, along with any advice or knowledge she could have given her. She was a psychic, not a medium, and so was her mom. Yet, for some reason the dead were communicating with her. *If* these women she'd been dreaming about were actually dead.

12

She stepped from the shower and hurried through her morning routine. If she moved quickly enough, she'd have time to stop by the Sheriff's Department and drop off her notes of last night's vision to Roy. Besides, if she allowed herself to finally wallow in her grief, she might not be able to make it through the day. Thanks to the horrific nightmares, her emotions were raw enough. Dwelling on the past would only complicate the present.

Redirecting her focus to the day ahead of her, she had herself ready in record time. She grabbed her notes, then went to her home office to make copies of them. After shoving the copies in her purse, she loaded her SUV with the baked goods she'd prepared last night in her basement kitchen, then headed off to see Sheriff Roy Hauserman.

Considering Wissota Falls was a small town, the worst crimes consisted of a few drunken brawls or occasional shoplifting down at the R & P, the local excuse for a grocery store. The Sheriff's Department had little activity, especially during the early morning hours, yet Roy was always there by seven a.m. No matter what time of day she stopped by, he always greeted her with welcoming arms.

She could use one of his big bear hugs this morning. A surrogate uncle and dear friend, he'd never once thought her eccentric. Instead, he'd always supported her, stood up for her, and offered her respect when others had called her crazy. A close friend to her mom and dad, Roy had been a staple in her life and she loved him dearly.

With a box of muffins in her hands, she shoved the door open with her hip. "Morning, Bev," she said, and placed the muffins on the receptionist's desk.

"Morning. My, these smell heavenly. Blueberry?"

"Yep, and cranberry, too."

Bev stood and peeked into the box. "Mmmm," she hummed, then released a deep sigh. "Tempting, but I'm on a diet."

"Again?" She eyed Bev, her perfectly styled red hair, make-up, tiny body, and abundant cleavage. "If you lose any more weight, you'll be nothing but walking boobs."

Bev laughed. "Hey, I'm pushing fifty and need to worry about my girlish figure."

"Are those muffins I smell?" Roy's deep voice came from his back office.

"I'll just remove temptation and head on back to see Roy," Celeste said with a smile, grabbed the box, then walked down the short, dismal corridor to the sheriff's office.

She rounded the corner and, for the first time since she'd woken this morning, relaxed. Roy's big grin splitting beneath his dark mustache and the affectionate gleam in his green eyes gave her a moment's worth of solace. The bright yellow walls she'd personally painted, the pale blue curtains on the window Bev had sewn, and the fragrant green plants resting on the desk and file cabinet offered her a warm reception. Then she remembered why she'd come to see him.

When her smile fell, Roy was around the desk, setting the box of muffins on the chair, and holding her in a matter of seconds. "What's the matter? Did you have another bad night?"

She nodded against his bulky chest.

"Honey, why don't you go see your doctor and have him prescribe you some sleeping pills?"

She stiffened and drew away. "No pills." She reached into her purse, then handed him her notes. She'd seen the way prescription drugs had affected her mother when she'd been sick, dying, and it hadn't been pretty. The drugs had a side effect that didn't work well on someone with psychic abilities.

Understanding softened the concern in his eyes. He nodded, then leaned against his desk and read her notes. The fine lines around his eyes deepened when he cringed. "I'm praying these are just nightmares and not your gift telling you something," he said, waving the papers in the air.

"Me too."

He opened the file cabinet and drew out a manila folder. "I'll put these with the others you gave me, and hope to God I don't have to look at them again."

If only she could be so lucky. Every time she closed her eyes she saw violence, causing ripples of dread and horror to course through her body and lodge deep within her soul. "Can't you do something?" she begged. "Send out a search party, look—"

He shook his head. "Look where? Every one of your visions takes place in the woods. I don't know if you've noticed, but we're surrounded by thousands of acres of the stuff."

She moved the box of muffins to the desk, then sagged into the chair opposite him and held her head in her hands, knowing he was right, hating that he was right. She couldn't expect him to send men on a wild goose chase, especially when she wasn't even sure if her visions were actually a third eye into the past, present, or future, or if they were just a case of plain old nightmares. Until four nights ago, she'd never once dreamed of anything heinous. She'd helped people she knew with finding a missing ring, or a lost dog—not dead bodies. Maybe she *was* eccentric, or maybe she was just crazy.

He leaned against the desk again. "I swear to you, if you give me something to indicate a specific locale, like a road sign, mile marker, billboard...I'll go out and look myself."

Tears stung her eyes, and she offered him a watery smile. "Thanks. And I know you're right. I just want the nightmares to stop. I want my normal life back."

"Don't you mean boring?" he asked quietly, a small smile lessening the minor insult.

"Boring? I...I'm not boring," she sputtered, and rose from the chair. She had a good life. Maybe not the most exciting, but she was...content. So what if living in Wissota Falls and running her dad's diner wasn't exactly where she'd expected to be at this point in her life. So what if her best friend happened to be a fifty-two-year old sheriff. She still had her brother and her baking.

God, she was boring and...lonely.

She moved to the fern resting on the file cabinet, and plucked a dead strand. "Normal, boring, or whatever you want to call it, beats the hell out of what I've been dealing with these past four nights." She threw the strand in the trash can. "Don't you water your plants?"

"The plants are Bev's job. Don't go changing the subject." He released a deep breath. "I didn't mean to say that your life is boring, but you're young. You should be out there dating, or doing whatever it is young people do for fun."

She'd had plenty of fun before leaving Madison, where she'd earned her degree at the University of Wisconsin. After college she'd taken a great job at an accounting firm. But family duty had forced her home. While she had no regrets in coming back to help her dad and brother take care of her sick mom, she hadn't planned on the move becoming permanent.

"Well," she said with a shrug. "There's not a whole lot of men to pick from around here. Besides, the diner keeps me busy."

"And now you have the nightmares to use as an excuse."

She stared at him, shocked by their entire conversation. He'd never told her how to live her life, and had only offered advice when she'd asked. A little annoyed, more with herself for not following her own dreams when she'd had the chance, she ignored the slight dig. "I better get going."

"Look, I'm sorry, I shouldn't have said—"

"No, it's okay. You're right." She forced a smile when she caught the worry lining his eyes and face again.

He didn't seem to buy her acquiescence as a frown creased his forehead drawing his bushy eyebrows together. "You gonna be okay? Maybe you should have Will stay with you for a few nights."

Her brother lived in the apartment above her detached garage. She liked her privacy, and didn't want Will invading her space, or knowing about the nightmares. He had enough on his mind.

"Sure, I'll talk to him. But don't say anything about these visions to him, okay? I don't want him worrying." She looked at her watch. "It's getting late, I've really gotta go. I don't want you to have to send a couple of cruisers down to The Sugar

Shack because people are rioting over not getting their breakfast."

He didn't smile at her lame joke as he walked with her out of the office. "You call if you need me, okay?"

"I will. But if something does happen, if somebody discovers..." She trailed off, not wanting to say aloud what she knew in her heart. Four women were dead.

He stopped and turned to her before reaching the reception area. "You have my word."

"Thank you. You're a good man for believing in a kook like me."

"Roy, I've got Ed on the phone for you," Bev shouted from around the corner.

"Why didn't he use his radio?" he asked as he approached the lobby.

Bev shrugged. "Don't know. But, for whatever reason, he sounds all shook up."

"He always does lately," he said with disgust.

Celeste grabbed his arm. "Go easy on him. It's only been a month since his wife lost the baby."

Regret creased his face as he rested a big hand on her shoulder. "You're right. Thank you for reminding me not to be such a bull-headed jackass."

"I remind you all time, and I never get a thank you," Bev huffed, and handed him the phone.

His mustache twitched as he hid a smile. "I'll check up on you later. And you're not *that* kooky," he added before he took the call from Ed.

With a genuine smile, she waved good-bye, then headed out the door. She had hungry customers to feed. She just hoped to God they'd be enough of a distraction from the visions haunting her mind.

Ian Scott scanned the files containing the case John Kain had recently closed. He had to hand it to the guy, every last detail had been accounted for, every last "i" dotted and "t" crossed. Not that John's meticulous eye for detail surprised him. The man was beyond methodical. His precision, discipline, and logical approach to situations were what had drawn Ian to recruit John to CORE, Criminal Observance Resolution and Evidence. His baby. His business. His personal private agency where he could weave his agents into the criminal world and take down the bad guys without being stonewalled by the bullshit red tape that government agencies and local law enforcement had to endure.

"Well done," he said, and tore his eyes from the report.

John, his top criminalist and a former special agent with the FBI, stood at the window, arms folded across his chest, his body rigid, his face haggard but clear of emotion. The man either had ice running through his veins or a heart of stone. What he'd witnessed during the last month would have had even the most seasoned professional either self-medicating with alcohol or popping prescription drugs courtesy of their shrink.

"Thank you, sir," John replied, as always, but this time, the tone in his voice lacked the normal respect. This time, there was an edge of sarcasm, so minute, if they weren't two of a kind, he'd likely have missed it. He didn't, and realized John needed some time to decompress. Maybe he'd made a mistake lending him to the local FBI office to track down the serial pedophile that had murdered and mutilated fourteen children from the Chicago area. Maybe it had been too soon to allow him to work with his former colleagues. He'd needed John on this case, though. He was the best of the best, and Chicago was Ian's hometown. He'd grown tired of seeing the victims splashed on the evening news.

"Why don't you take some time off? I'll arrange for you to stay at the company condo in Scottsdale. The golf courses are excellent, and the weather is mild this time of the year."

A brief flicker of interest flashed in John's eyes, then faded when the phone rang. "Excuse me." Ian reached for his private line. "Scott," he answered, clutching the phone against his ear.

Five people had this number, and they only called at scheduled times. Now was not one of them.

"It's Roy, and I've got a hell of a situation."

He glanced to John and covered the phone with his hand, fighting the fear. Which was ridiculous. Ryker was dead and no longer a threat, he'd seen to it. Personally. "John, please step outside. But don't go far," he added, because if something bad had happened in Wissota Falls, he needed one of his best agents there. Scottsdale would have to wait.

John nodded and did as he'd requested. Once the door quietly clicked behind him, Ian shoved the phone back to his ear. "Celeste?"

"She's fine, she's safe, but she's involved."

"Details."

"I've got four dead bodies. My deputy found one when he got out of his car to take a leak in the woods. When we canvassed the area we found three others."

"Did you call in DCI?" The Wisconsin Department of Criminal Investigation would lend a hand in a crime like this, but he didn't want a pissing match if CORE became involved. While many state investigation agencies, even the FBI, had enlisted the help of his agency, he hadn't worked with DCI yet and wasn't sure if he wanted to, especially if Celeste was somehow involved. He needed one of his men there. They were his eyes and ears, and because they'd been hand-picked by him, he knew they'd do their job without fail.

"No. But CSU from Eau Claire is on its way. My boys aren't trained or experienced enough to deal with this."

The rough edge in Roy's tone made him pause. He'd known the man for over thirty years, and he didn't like the sound of his voice. "What do you see?"

"Shit that I haven't since...since Janice."

Celeste's mother. Gripping the phone tight, he tried to gather his control. "What *exactly* do you see?"

Wind whipped over the phone line, and he knew Roy was on the move, could hear the crunching of leaves, the crack of sticks. "Four women, nude, battered...dead. Looks like they're all decomposing at the same time."

"*At the same time?*"

"I can't be sure, until the ME does an autopsy," Roy added, "but from the looks of the women, that's my guess."

"And Celeste is involved how?" Even as he asked the question, he already knew the answer. He'd known her mother, what she'd been capable of, what she'd been able to see when no one else could.

"For the past four nights she had visions of women being murdered. They were vague, every one of them happening in the woods, and we've got acres here. I wouldn't have even known where to start."

"I understand." That was the problem with psychics sometimes. They saw things, things that will happen or actually had happened, but without a surefire locale, it was the clichéd needle in a haystack. "I'll send one of my agents. Have one of your deputies meet him at the airstrip outside of Eau Claire. He'll be there in about an hour."

"Who am I expecting?"

He stared at his closed office door where just outside John waited. The criminalist had spent a month dealing with the deaths of children at the hands of a sick bastard. He needed to decompress, but Ian had no choice. All of his other agents were on assignment.

Moving his gaze from the door, he said, "John Kain."

"Got it. I'll call you tonight. Seven sharp."

"Seven, it is. And Roy, use Celeste on this. If she's anything like her mother..."

"Your agent will cooperate with a psychic?"

No, Kain did not believe in psychics. He believed in facts, evidence, hardcore science. In this instance, though, he'd have no choice. Ian would see to it. "Trust me. He'll cooperate."

CHAPTER 2

LESS THAN TWO hours later, John Kain knelt, resting his forearm on his thigh as he studied one of the four victims. Bruises marred her flesh, her inner thighs, her face and chest, while her mouth gaped open as if she'd died screaming. The thin line of purple running around her neck was telling. She'd been strangled. Beaten, raped, then strangled. Just like the other three.

Roy, the sheriff who'd reminded him of Paul Bunyan, minus the ax and blue ox, came up beside him. "What are you thinking?"

John stood, then scanned the area, the dense woods, the highway where the deputies had set up a road block. The smooth asphalt was littered with police cruisers, several CSU vans, and maybe a half-dozen deputies. "I can't be sure, but I spoke with...Mitchell?"

"Yeah." The sheriff nodded. "He's the lead with Eau Claire's CSU team."

"Mitchell tentatively confirmed your suspicions, but will know more during the autopsies."

"Shit."

"My exact thought. You're in a heap of it." And he'd just plowed through his own pile in Chicago, the stench still lingering, still fresh.

When he'd joined CORE, he'd known he would see just as

21

much as he had when he'd been with the FBI, but Ian had promised downtime in between cases, something he'd never had with the Bureau. Something he needed now. What he'd witnessed while working with the Chicago PD and FBI Field Office would haunt him for a lifetime. And as pissed as he was about having a mini-vacation dangled in front of him, then quickly pulled away with one simple phone call, he still had a job to do.

He would never say no to Ian Scott. Ian had resurrected him from the dead, had given him a job, a lucrative income, and the ability to do the only thing he knew how to—catch killers no one else could.

Mitchell approached. "We covered a fifty-yard radius so far, and didn't find any of the victims' clothing, but," he said and cocked a brow. "We got a footprint about seven yards from where the three bodies were found, along with a button and a lighter scattered on the trail. Not much to go on, but considering how clean the site is...maybe we'll get lucky and find a print."

"Thanks, Mitchell," Roy said.

"After we move the bodies, I'm going to have my guys do another sweep, take the radius out another—"

"I wouldn't bother," John interrupted.

Mitchell plucked off his Latex gloves. "Why's that?"

"You have one body here." He pointed to the woman he'd just examined, her pale body stark white against the dark earth and brown leaves. "And three clustered together, what, thirty, forty yards away? He kept the clothes. You won't find anything if you expand your search."

Mitchell crossed his arms over his chest and sent him a "you're so full of shit" look. "And you know this how?"

John turned to the sheriff, ignoring Mitchell. "No disrespect, but you're small time here. I imagine you don't have the manpower to patrol this area very often. If our guy scoped the area, he'd know his window of opportunity. It took me twelve and a half minutes to walk to where the three women were found. I'd imagine it would take our guy about the same,